Scaredy Smurf
Makes a Friend

by Peyo

Ready-to-Read

Simon Spotlight
New York London Toronto Sydney New Delhi

SIMON SPOTLIGHT
An imprint of Simon & Schuster Children's Publishing Division
1230 Avenue of the Americas, New York, New York 10020
© Peyo - 2013 - Licensed through Lafig Belgium - www.smurf.com. All Rights Reserved.
For information about special discounts for bulk purchases, please contact Simon & Schuster Special Sales at
1-866-506-1949 or business@simonandschuster.com. The Simon & Schuster Speakers Bureau can bring
authors to your live event. For more information or to book an event contact the
Simon & Schuster Speakers Bureau at 1-866-248-3049 or visit our website at www.simonspeakers.com.
Manufactured in the United States of America 0513 LAK
First Edition
2 4 6 8 10 9 7 5 3 1
ISBN 978-1-4424-7366-9 (pbk)
ISBN 978-1-4424-7367-6 (hc)

t is really great to be a Smurf!
Smurfs spend a lot of time having fun,
playing, and relaxing.

But there is one Smurf who is different from all the other Smurfs. His name is Scaredy Smurf, and as you might guess from his name, he's afraid of just about everything!

While the other Smurfs laugh and
play in the pond,
Scaredy Smurf is afraid of the water!
He will not even jump in!

While the other Smurfs love to go hiking up the mountain, Scaredy Smurf stays back. He is too scared to be up so high. What if he were to fall down the mountain?

Scaredy Smurf is happiest when he is by himself.

One day Jokey Smurf decided to play a trick on Scaredy Smurf. After all, Jokey Smurf loves playing tricks!

He found a scary monster costume and put it on. He knew that Scaredy Smurf would be so scared when he saw him!

Jokey Smurf waited for Scaredy Smurf.
Finally Scaredy Smurf walked by . . .
and Jokey jumped out of the doorway
dressed as the monster and let out a
loud roar!
Scaredy Smurf was terrified!

Scaredy Smurf ran away and hid in
a barrel. The other Smurfs saw him
and laughed at him.
"What a chicken!" shouted one Smurf.
Scaredy Smurf felt very ashamed.

Scaredy Smurf decided to go home
so he would not have to listen
to the other Smurfs laughing at him
anymore. He just wanted to be alone.

But when he got home, Scaredy Smurf
realized he was not alone!
There was a spider waiting for him
in the middle of the room . . . and to
Scaredy Smurf, the spider looked huge!

Scaredy Smurf jumped on top of a table.

But the spider was scared too!

She was scared of Scaredy Smurf!

She ran away and hid under a cabinet.

Scaredy Smurf looked closely at the spider. Her eyes were shining under the cabinet. As he watched her, Scaredy realized that the spider was scared, too. Suddenly Scaredy didn't feel as scared anymore!

Come out. I am not going to hurt you,"
caredy Smurf said gently to the
pider. Carefully the spider left her
iding place . . . and met Scaredy
murf! And neither one was very
cary after all!

Scaredy Smurf realized that he liked
having the spider around!
She kept him company as he swept
the floor . . .

And she played on the floor while he read a book in his rocking chair. "Wow! I have a pet spider!" Scaredy Smurf said happily.

But the next day Scaredy Smurf
worried that his pet spider wasn't very
happy. "Is she bored?" he wondered as
he watched her look out the window.

Then he decided that perhaps she
was hungry. Scaredy Smurf wasn't sure
what spiders liked to eat.
So he decided to take her on a walk.

Scaredy Smurf was surprised by the reaction he and his pet spider got around the village. Every Smurf was terrified of the spider! "It's a monster!" cried the first Smurf who saw them.

Smurfette screamed when she saw the
spider. Another Smurf burst into tears!
And one ran away, screaming all the way.

Finally Scaredy Smurf couldn't take
it anymore.
"Stop it!" he shouted!
"Stop smurfing at my pet spider!
She is very gentle!"

But the Smurfs would not listen.
They were too scared!
"She belongs in the woods!" the other
Smurfs insisted.

"I think it would be best if you returned
to the woods,"
Scaredy Smurf said sadly to the spider.
"The other Smurfs are just
too scared of you."
The spider understood.

Scaredy Smurf walked the spider back
to the woods.
"Good-bye and good luck!" he told her.
"It was really nice meeting you!
Please come back and visit me!"

Papa Smurf watched as Scaredy
said good-bye to the spider.
"Weren't you afraid of that spider,
Scaredy Smurf?" asked Papa Smurf.

"I was a little bit scared at first," Scaredy Smurf admitted.
"But then I got to know her, and I realized she wasn't scary."
"You put your fear aside and made a great new friend,"
Papa Smurf said. "I am proud of you!"
Scaredy Smurf felt great!

"You were all scared of the spider, but Scaredy Smurf was brave!" Papa told the other Smurfs. "Everyone is scared sometimes. Remember that the next time you want to tease someone."
It was a good lesson for all the Smurfs!